DATE DUE

JAN 3			
OCT 03			
DEC 15			
DEC 2 1			
		Demco

Demco

THE FERRET

BY
JANE DUDEN

EDITED BY
JULIE BACH

Roosevelt Elementary
ISD 706

New York

LIBRARY OF CONGRESS CATALOGING IN PUBLICATION DATA

Duden, Jane.
   The ferret

   (Wildlife, habits & habitat)
   Includes index.
   SUMMARY: Examines the physical characteristics, behavior, and natural environment of the black-footed ferret, with an emphasis on its endangered status and the
efforts of scientists to save it, and discusses ferrets in captivity.
   1. Black-footed ferret—Juvenile literature.   [1. Black-footed ferret.   2. Ferret.
3. Rare animals.   4. Wildlife conservation.]   I. Title.   II. Series.
QL737.C25D83   1990   599.74'447—dc20   89-28268
ISBN 0-89686-517-7

PHOTO CREDITS:

Cover: Wyoming Game & Fish Department: LuRay Parker
DRK Photo: (Stephen J. Krasemann) 39, 40; (Jeff Foott) 31
Wyoming Game & Fish Department: (LuRay Parker) 4, 8, 9, 11, 12, 15, 17, 19, 22, 23,
   24, 26, 28, 32, 35, 36, 45

Macmillan Publishing Company
866 Third Avenue
New York, NY 10022
Collier Macmillan Canada, Inc.

CRESTWOOD HOUSE

Printed in the United States of America
First Edition
10 9 8 7 6 5 4 3 2 1

TABLE OF CONTENTS

INTRODUCTION:

On September 25, 1981, John and Lucille Hogg awoke to the barking of their ranch dog, Shep. Snarling and shrieking pierced the darkness. Then all was quiet.

When the Wyoming sun came up, John went outside for a look. Shep had killed a furry, little, mask-faced creature. John thought it looked like a cross between a dachshund and a raccoon, or like a long-necked, oversized mink. Neither John nor Lucille had ever seen such an animal.

Lucille thought the little creature was unusual enough to be mounted. But the *taxidermist* in nearby Meeteetse, Wyoming, surprised the Hoggs. He told them that he thought Shep's *prey* might be a black-footed ferret, an animal so rare it was thought to be *extinct*! The animal was given to the local game warden who, in turn, gave it to the U.S. Fish and Wildlife Service. The U.S. Fish and Wildlife Service identified the animal as the black-footed ferret.

Shep's dead ferret created a big stir. Local and federal wildlife officials were called in. Ranchers and townspeople met with the Hoggs. An alert was sent out to find this rare animal. The search was on.

On October 29, 1981, a live black-footed ferret was spotted near Meeteetse. *Conservationists* were overjoyed. They began intensive ferret searches in the area. To the

During the early 1980s, sightings of wild ferrets became more and more rare.

best knowledge of scientists, the Meeteetse ferrets are the only known *colony* of black-footed ferrets in the world.

Researchers studying the ferret faced a big challenge. They had to "ferret out" the animal's secrets and unlock the keys to its survival. They wondered how many ferrets there were. What were the threats to ferrets in other areas? How could humans protect ferrets and help them increase their numbers?

The quest to save the ferrets has caused some tense moments. It could be called the environmental detective story of the 1980s. Many hope it will become the conservation success story of the century.

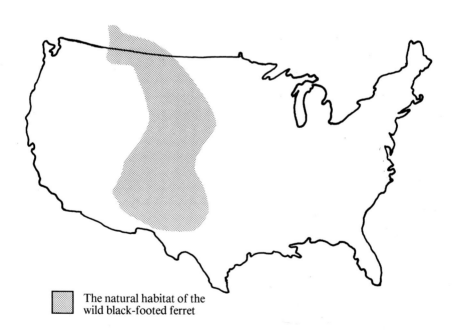

The natural habitat of the wild black-footed ferret

Black-footed ferrets (*Mustela nigripes*) are the rarest *mammals* in North America and perhaps in the world. They were thought to be extinct until the Wyoming ranch dog Shep discovered otherwise.

Mustela nigripes is an *endangered species* native to the plains and prairies of North America. It is not the same creature as its cousin *Mustela putorius,* the *domesticated* European ferret sold in pet stores, though they are similar.

Masked bandit

The name "ferret" comes from the Latin word *furritus,* which means little thief. The ferret has a black face mask. The animal once inhabited the Great Plains from southern Canada to west Texas, in all the same regions where prairie dogs were found. Prairie dogs are squirrel-like rodents that live in social groups called colonies.

The black-footed ferret is a member of the mammal group named *mustelids.* It is related to the mink and the weasel. Skunks, badgers, sea otters, and wolverines are other mustelids. All have long, slender bodies, short legs, rounded ears, and bright, buttonlike eyes. Mustelids have *scent glands* under their tails. Sharp claws, strong jaws, and large *canine teeth* make them well adapted for burrowing and eating meat.

Ferrets range in length from 18 to 24 inches. Their tails are about one-fourth of their total length. They weigh from two and a half to three and a half pounds. Males are somewhat larger than females.

A scientist displays a ferret's long, sharp canine teeth.

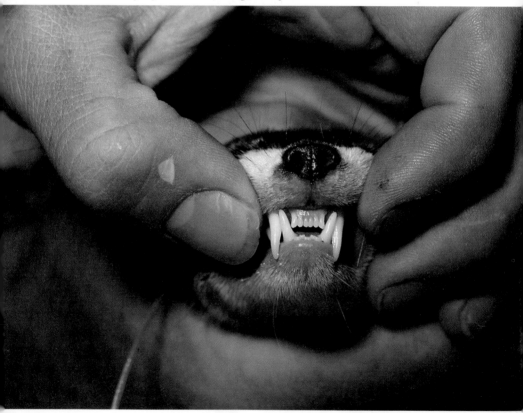

Its slender body lets the black-footed ferret slip easily through underground tunnels.

A prairie hunter

The black-footed ferret is a quick prairie hunter. It lives about five or six years in the wild.

The ferret is well adapted to its environment. Its slender body allows it to move easily in underground tunnels. Short legs and sharp-clawed paws are helpful for digging. Its short, sleek fur is a pale yellow-buff color that blends

9

in well with prairie soils and plants. The fur is lighter on the belly and nearly white on the forehead, *muzzle*, and throat. (Unlike a weasel's, the ferret's coat does not turn white in winter.) It has a black face mask and black feet. Its tail is black at the tip.

The ferret can stretch tall and thin on its hind legs to peer and sniff for food, sense danger, or search for a mate. Its legs are strong. The ferret can bound through summer prairie grass or winter snow. The ferret is *nocturnal*, or active at night. It has a good sense of smell for hunting in the dark or in underground tunnels. Large eyes and ears suggest it has the good hearing and sight of a hunter.

The prairie dog connection

Prairie dogs and ferrets have lived in the same areas for thousands of years. Ferret and prairie dog skeletons have been found in camps where *prehistoric* Indians lived. The Indians knew of the close tie between the two animals. Some Native Americans thought ferrets had special powers. Their stories about them suggest that ferrets have always been hard to find.

The colonies that prairie dogs live in are called *prairie dog towns*. The towns are the *habitat* of black-footed ferrets. The ferrets live and hunt there. Black-footed ferrets

10

Scientists have dug dirt tunnels for the black-footed ferrets in captivity.

will sometimes eat ground squirrels, deer mice, birds, and cottontail rabbits. But it has been estimated that 90 percent of their diet is prairie dog.

Ferrets do not build their own *burrows*. They move into old prairie dog burrows. The burrows stay cool during hot, dry summers. They are warm in winter. Some burrows have two or more entrances, so ferrets or prairie dogs can escape if they are being chased. Most of the burrows have small rooms off to the sides where ferrets can build nests. Here they sleep, hide their food, and give birth to their *kits*, or young.

Unfortunately, prairie dog towns have been nearly wiped out in six of the twelve states and in the one Cana-

dian province where ferrets were thought to have originally lived. Prairie dogs like deep, level soils for their homes. Farmers and ranchers like those same soils for grazing cattle and raising crops. They do not want prairie dogs digging burrows and eating the grass. Since the turn of the century, landowners have been poisoning, gassing, or shooting prairie dogs. That means ferret habitats have been greatly reduced. Remaining habitats are limited. From the turn of the century until the environmental movement of the 1960s, people were not as concerned about animals and the environment as they are today. Had they known then what we know now, they might not have destroyed so many prairie dog colonies.

CHAPTER TWO:

Studies of the Meeteetse ferrets have provided new information about ferret habits and needs. For example, they are probably less active in winter than in summer. They live and hunt alone. They avoid other ferrets except in the breeding season and during the summer, when the female is raising her young. Ferrets are seen with any regularity only when the female and young are present.

Ferret tracks usually don't cross because each animal stays in its own territory. But in mid-March, their tracks begin to overlap. This is a clue that mating season has begun.

Ferrets rely on prairie dogs like the one shown here for their survival.

13

Ferrets usually produce *litters* of one to five kits each May or June. Male ferrets are called *hobs*, or dogs. They do not stay around after mating or help in raising the young. The females, or *jills,* are secretive, careful mothers.

Fast-growing ferret kits

Ferret babies are born tiny and helpless, with eyes tightly shut. Their thin white fuzz has no markings. Their only food is their mother's milk. They stay underground in the burrows until they are several weeks old. Sometimes a mother carries her kits by the backs of their necks to new burrows. She always sniffs the air and looks around for any signs of danger before leaving her burrow.

When the kits are about eight weeks old, in mid-July, they begin to eat meat. But they stay safely in the burrow when the mother leaves to hunt. Soon she begins coaxing them out of the burrow to play.

By now they have the same markings as their mother. They totter behind her like the cars of a toy train. Soon they are braver and stronger. They bound through the grass, single file, following her. She may lead them to a burrow where she has left a dead prairie dog for them to eat.

By the time a ferret is eight weeks old, its coat has the same markings as its mother.

Ferrets at play

Ferret kits play much like kittens. They come above ground at night or in the early morning to play around their burrows. They chase flies and play tag with each other. They follow their tails in circles, dance on their tiptoes, and run backward. They nip at each other's ears and try to topple their mothers with playful leaps.

By August, some kits look full grown. Some weigh as much as their mothers. But they aren't ready yet to hunt by themselves. Long after they stop nursing, they depend on the mother for meals of prairie dog.

Hunters in training

The mother and kits stay together through the summer. The kits must learn important skills. They are taught to watch out for hawks or bobcats that could eat them. They must learn to hunt, for their survival depends on it.

The *instinct* to hunt is powerful, and the kits learn fast. They first "hunt" rocks or flowers. It is a game for them, but good practice. They crouch and stare, then sneak up and pounce. They practice on grasshoppers and mice. Their skills and confidence grow with practice. Soon they successfully hunt prairie dogs.

Leaving the colony

By late summer, the kits stay in separate burrows during the day. At first the mothers still bring them food. But each night they gather together to hunt. Before long, the young ferrets hunt alone and the family doesn't live together at all.

By fall the ferrets are independent. Some leave the area where they were born to live and mate in other prairie dog colonies. But with so few prairie dog towns left, they may find it hard to make it safely to new ones. They may find no prairie dogs to eat and may have to eat less suitable food. They may not find burrows in which to escape from enemies and harsh weather.

Nocturnal animals, young wild ferrets gather together to hunt at night.

Dangers
to ferrets

A *free-ranging* (living in the wild) ferret faces many risks. It stays alive by killing sharp-toothed prairie dogs that are often twice its size. That means many battle injuries and scars. It also has to dodge *predators* that would enjoy a ferret meal. Coyotes, foxes, badgers, owls, eagles, and hawks are some hunters of ferrets. Domestic cats and dogs, like Shep, will go after ferrets, too.

Death from disease can threaten both ferrets and their main food supply, prairie dogs. *Sylvatic plague* and *canine distemper* are two diseases that can wipe out a ferret population. Sylvatic plague can sweep through prairie dog towns, killing the food that ferrets depend on. Canine distemper is the viral disease that is dangerous to pet dogs and cats. It is carried in nature by skunks, foxes, coyotes, and other animals. It is also carried on the shoes, clothes, or hands of humans who own dogs. It can even be spread through the air.

The Meeteetse ferrets live in several prairie dog towns. Still they are close enough to one another that any disease could easily be spread. Prairie dogs or ferrets could carry disease from town to town.

Another danger to such a small population of ferrets is *inbreeding*. There is little variety in *genes* when a small number of animals are mating. Genes are units that pass on inherited traits to offspring. A limited *gene pool* en-

When handling wild ferrets, scientists wear masks to reduce the chance of spreading any disease to the ferrets.

courages weaknesses or defects to show up in newborns. The ones not well suited for survival will die easily. Some may even stop reproducing. When this happens to a *species,* the line between survival and extinction is thin.

Habitat loss is the ferret's worst enemy. Without a suitable home, there can be no free-ranging ferrets. Loss of the ferret's main prey also is a very serious threat.

19

CHAPTER THREE:

The first two sightings of black-footed ferrets ever reported were in Wyoming. And that is where the last known black-footed ferrets in the world were discovered as well. They were discovered near Meeteetse, Wyoming, and the U.S. Fish and Wildlife Service (US FWS) and the state of Wyoming became partners in protecting the species. Under the Endangered Species Act of 1973, the Wyoming Game & Fish Department formed a *recovery* plan that would help ferrets increase their numbers in captivity until they could survive on their own. The plan required capturing a few of the Meeteetse ferrets for breeding in captivity.

Almost extinct

The black-footed ferret always may have been rare. It was first reported and described by the artist John James Audubon in the mid 1800s. It baffled scientists for a long time. No one reported seeing it again until 26 years later. In other words, the black-footed ferret was rarely observed in the wild for nearly one hundred years. Little was known of its habits or habitat.

Then in 1964, a ferret mother and her young were found in a prairie dog town in western South Dakota. People thought that those South Dakota ferrets were the last ones in the world. They were put on the U.S. Endangered Species list in 1966. In the early 1970s, nine of the animals were captured. They were taken to Patuxent Wildlife Research Center in Laurel, Maryland. People hoped more black-footed ferrets would be born. But every litter was dead at birth. The last remaining ferret from those nine died in 1979.

In 1972, a drowned ferret was discovered in a livestock watering tank in Wyoming. Wildlife researchers searched the area, hoping to find more. But after the last Patuxent ferret died in 1979, many researchers thought the black-footed ferret was extinct—until John and Lucille Hogg's dog Shep killed one in 1981. The rest of the story is unfolding daily.

A tough study

Scientists cannot study an animal that cannot be found. But finding a ferret isn't easy. Ferrets are nocturnal. They spend most of their lives underground. They come out for only short periods, to hunt and find new burrows or mates. They are secretive and solitary.

Even so, *biologists* have ways to locate and count ferrets and observe their behavior. The Meeteetse research team drove through prairie dog colonies at night. They shone spotlights over the ground. Just as a deer's eyes shine in the headlights of a car, a ferret's eyes reflect a bright green color. Late summer and early fall are the best

A wild black-footed ferret cautiously peeks out of its burrow.

times to locate ferrets with spotlights. That's when the
young begin venturing out of their burrows.

Researchers also look for signs left by ferrets. Tracks in
the snow show their paths from one prairie dog burrow to
another. Marks can also show where a ferret has killed a
prairie dog and dragged it to another burrow. Ferret diggings are another sign. Ferrets drag dirt out of the ground
and string it out in a long thin pile. Researchers tracked

one ferret that made four diggings in one night. It had dragged 90 pounds of dirt to the surface.

A few ferrets in the Meeteetse colony were trapped safely and fitted with radio collars. Then they were released. Radio signals from the collar helped pinpoint a ferret's location when it was active above ground.

Researchers watched ferrets in daylight with *spotting scopes* and binoculars. They took photographs when ferrets ventured outside.

Scientists place a radio collar on a ferret to track its movements underground.

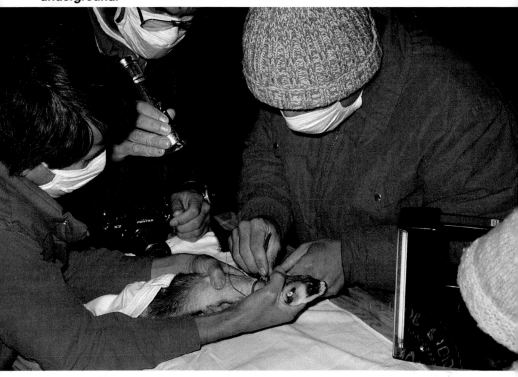

In search of black-footed ferrets

Still hoping to find other populations of this rare species, the Meeteetse researchers decided they needed all the help they could get.

After trapping a ferret, researchers take the animal back to their lab where it will be kept safely with other ferrets.

In January 1984, *Handbook of Methods for Locating Black-Footed Ferrets* was printed to help in the search for ferrets. The book's photographs and diagrams of ferrets and their activities help people search for ferrets. It can be ordered from the U.S. Bureau of Land Management in Cheyenne, Wyoming.

In addition, a $5,000 reward was offered for verified black-footed ferret sightings. Conservation International, a division of the New York Zoological Society, offered the reward. People all over the United States began to get involved in protecting the ferrets.

Many private and public agencies donated money. The Black-Footed Ferret Trust Fund has been established by the National Fish and Wildlife Foundation, the U.S. Fish and Wildlife Service, the Wyoming Wildlife Federation, and the Wyoming Game & Fish Department. The first money in this fund came from the sale of a painting, *The New Generation*. The painting showed the first ferrets born in captivity.

Ferret boosters everywhere

Young people also did what they could to help. Thousands of Wyoming schoolchildren entered the first Annual Black-Footed Ferret Art Contest in 1984. They hoped for a chance to see some of the rare animals that were the subjects of their posters.

The town of Meeteetse went ferret-crazy. They adopted the ferrets. They made a sign proclaiming Meeteetse to be "Ferret Capital of the World." Lucille's Cafe, owned by Lucille Hogg, began selling ferret T-shirts, mugs, and caps. The town formed a women's softball team called— what else?—the Ferrettes.

In 1984, many ferrets were trapped and placed in captivity in order to start a captive breeding program.

In 1984, the sixth graders of Allen Creek School in Pittsford, New York, also became ferret boosters. They raised $112 and donated the money to the Wyoming Game & Fish Department's ferret program.

Milo Bassett of Star Valley, Wyoming, was so interested in black-footed ferrets that he started a ferret fan club. Milo and the other members of the club felt that more people should become involved with ferret research. Then this rare animal could be saved.

CHAPTER FOUR:

Because it is the rarest mammal in North America, and perhaps the world, the ferret deserves all the protection we can give it. And since humans indirectly caused the ferret's endangered status, it is up to each and every one of us to save them.

The population takes a nosedive

In 1984, the wild ferret population in Meeteetse was 129. So plans were made that year to start a *captive breeding* program. A few ferrets would be taken into captivity in hopes of breeding more ferrets. Having a second ferret population separate from the Meeteetse wild ferrets was

Researchers keep track of the captive ferrets' activities with video monitors.

good insurance. If the wild ferrets were wiped out by a disaster, there would still be ferrets elsewhere. Sybille (pronounced sah-BEEL) Wildlife Research and Conservation Education Center was chosen to house the new population. It already had an expert staff and was remote and safe. A design for a new building was drawn up.

But in the summer of 1985, before the captive breeding

28

program began, a crisis occurred. Fleas carrying sylvatic plague showed up in a routine sample of Meeteetse prairie dogs. When sylvatic plague kills prairie dogs, ferrets lose their main source of food.

Experts took no chances. They spent $20,000 and sprayed almost 100,000 prairie dog holes on 6,200 acres to control the fleas. It was perhaps the world's largest flea dusting outside a city in history. They took six ferrets into captivity, hoping to breed more. Captive breeding had been talked about since ferrets were discovered near Meeteetse. If the Meeteetse ferrets were indeed the world's only ones, it might be the last chance to recover the species.

In late summer, there were more signs of trouble. Ferret counts kept dropping. Spotlighters found only 13 litters. In 1984, they had found 25 litters. Breeding was down. Worst of all, the six captured ferrets all died from canine distemper. Experts were sure the ferrets had caught the virus before they were captured. That meant the only known colony of black-footed ferrets was in the middle of a canine distemper outbreak. The virus already had proven deadly to black-footed ferrets. (The first four Patuxent ferrets had been given *vaccines*. They were so sensitive to the vaccine that the small amount of live virus in it killed them.) If the Meeteetse ferrets had not been discovered in 1981, it is extremely likely that they would have died in 1985 from canine distemper and passed, unwatched, into extinction.

A difficult decision

The Wyoming Game & Fish Department and the U.S. Fish and Wildlife Service faced an emergency. They decided on August 27, 1985, to remove all the known black-footed ferrets from their habitat. It was the most difficult decision made by a state wildlife agency during this century. Every known member of the species would be placed in captivity. The survival or extinction of a species would be in the hands of a state wildlife agency. The odds were against it. The captive breeding facility had not yet been built. Captive breeding was very expensive. Funds would be needed. And black-footed ferrets had never before been born and raised successfully in captivity.

Meeteetse ferrets captured

Temporary facilities were readied at Wyoming's Sybille Wildlife Research and Conservation Education Center and the University of Wyoming. Biologists, *veterinarians*, and other experts were on hand.

Between October 1985 and September 1986, 17 ferrets were taken into captivity. The last known member at Meeteetse was captured in February 1987. That brought

A scientist coaxes a ferret out of its burrow.

the total to 18 animals. The only known free-ranging ferret population was lost. But with these 18 captive ferrets, the species had a chance for survival.

The ferret makes a comeback

After teetering on the brink of extinction, the black-footed ferret is making a comeback. In 1986, two litters were born at Sybille Wildlife Research and Conservation Education Center. They brought the total number of black-footed ferrets in captivity up to 25. Becky and Jenny were the proud mothers of the first ferrets ever born in captivity.

January 1988 brought a setback. A four-year-old female named Willa died of cancer at Sybille. Willa's genes were a great loss to such a small breeding population. Her ovaries and eggs were removed upon her death. Researchers tried to fertilize the eggs with frozen sperm from a male black-footed ferret. It did not work. Research is now being conducted to perfect this technique.

But later that year, 34 young were added in an outstanding breeding season. It was especially good news because the young females produced from the 1987 litters had bred and produced litters of their own.

A captive ferret studies its new environment.

33

Dividing the colony

Experts decided it was now time to split the breeding colony. Two zoos were selected. Dividing the ferrets would spread the costs of the captive breeding program. It would also protect the ferrets if a catastrophe occurred. If fire or disease swept Sybille, the world would have no black-footed ferrets.

In October 1986, eight young ferrets were flown to a new home at the National Zoological Park's Conservation and Research Center in Front Royal, Virginia. Eight more ferrets went to the Henry Doorly Zoo in Omaha, Nebraska, in December. The ferrets cannot be seen by the public. The two sites, along with Sybille, continue the captive breeding of the endangered species. The new zoos receive young ferrets born in captivity. All the founding animals—the original ferrets captured at Meeteetse—remain at Sybille. Additional facilities will be selected as the population increases. Ferret experts hope to have a total of five facilities.

The 1989 breeding season produced 72 young at Sybille and 6 at Front Royal. No young were born at Omaha in 1989. The ferret experts celebrated. From a total of only 18 ferrets, the world's ferret population had grown to 120 living ferrets. It was nearly back to the high of 1984.

These forty-seven-day-old ferrets have grown strong and healthy in their controlled environment.

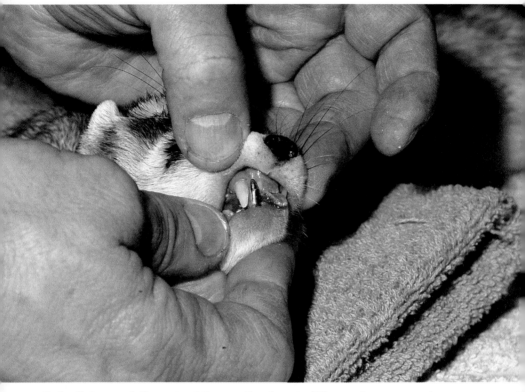

Scientists carefully protect the captive ferrets. When a ferret named Dean broke a tooth, a doctor replaced it with a gold crown.

Rare care

All the captive ferrets receive the best care. In 1987, a male ferret named Dean had a broken canine or "eye" tooth. It could have caused a dangerous infection. Dr. Peter Emily of Denver, Colorado, performed a root canal operation. He fitted Dean's tooth with a gold crown.

Dean is now not only one of the rarest mammals, but also the rarest animal to be fitted with a gold crown.

The ferrets are kept in pens. Passages lead to darkened nest boxes that are as much like their natural homes as possible. Caretakers are kept to a minimum. In most cases, the ferrets are disturbed only once a day, for feeding. Anyone who goes near the ferrets is required to shower and wear clean overalls and a surgical mask. Shoes are washed with disinfectant. No chances are taken for the deadly canine distemper virus to find its way to the captive ferrets.

A return to the wild?

The goal of the Black-Footed Ferret Recovery Plan is for ferrets to live again in all the states where they used to live. Captive breeding is the tool. Researchers hope to have 200 breeding pairs, or 500 ferrets, by 1991. If that happens, ferrets will be *reintroduced*, or released, back into the wild. By 2010, scientists hope to have at least ten wild colonies. They also hope to have 1,500 free-ranging and breeding ferrets.

Disease research continues. Back in the wild, ferrets will need disease protection. They will also need to be "trained" in the art of being wild ferrets. No longer will food drop into their cages. Researchers plan to build prairie dog towns. Ferrets can then learn to rely on their instincts and develop hunting skills. They expect reintroduced ferrets to need a little extra food and care at first.

Ferrets need prairie dogs for survival. A good release site will have active prairie dog towns. It will be a place where prairie dogs are accepted as important to the web of life. The cooperation and support of landowners is necessary.

Meeteetse, Wyoming, is the first planned release site. Come 1991, many ferrets will be packed up and set free.

Safe but not secure

The real measure of success will come when black-footed ferrets are taken off the endangered species list. When ferrets are again living and thriving in their twelve-state range, we will have a success story. Even then, ferrets will face risks. Exploring and drilling for oil in western areas could destroy prairie dog colonies and ferret habitats. So could digging new coal fields to supply our country's energy needs. Ranchers, oil companies, and other people are encouraged to use the land wisely to avoid harming the ferrets.

Many conservation groups, universities, scientists, private citizens, and government agencies are working together to help all endangered species. They support research with money. They know that their dedication and cooperation can give these animals a chance to live naturally where they belong, in their wild state.

When the ferret population has grown, scientists hope to free the captive ferrets and watch them prosper in the wild.

The European ferret is often domesticated and kept as a pet.

CHAPTER FIVE:

Wildlife lovers are working hard to protect the endangered black-footed ferret. In the meantime, common ferrets are catching on with pet owners. In the United States, about one million ferrets are now kept as pets. Young, hand-raised ferrets make clean, quiet, and affectionate pets. They can be housebroken to a litter box.

Ferrets kept as pets in the United States belong to a domesticated species, the European ferret. This species has been imported into the United States by the pet industry. The European ferret has a dark mask, dark feet, and an all-black tail. It is plumper and has more fur than the native black-footed ferret.

While its curious, alert nature, long body, and strong, short legs make a European ferret look like a hunter, it is not one. If released in the wild or lost, a pet ferret probably will suffer and starve. Many ferret owners put collars, name tags, or bells on their ferrets to identify them as pets. They can be returned to safety in case they become lost.

Pet ferrets are active, intelligent animals that can live from eight to eleven years. If you think a ferret is the pet for you, shop at a well-recommended pet store. Or choose a local breeder from an ad in the newspaper. Knowledgeable sellers are important. They can answer questions and help you select a healthy, high-quality ferret.

In the late 1980s, the average price of a ferret from a pet store was about $80 to $100. Breeders often charged slightly more. The cage, toys, food, and equipment cost about half the purchase price.

Packed with personality

Pet ferrets combine the best traits of cats and dogs and eliminate the worst. They are playful, like kittens, but they do not claw the furniture. They are almost as affectionate as dogs, but they do not bark or growl at guests. They do not need to be walked in all kinds of weather. They usually get along well with other pets in the home.

Ferrets are curious. They explore every nook and cranny. They crawl into the oddest places. This curiosity can also spell disaster. Ferret owners have searched for their pets only to find them under or inside refrigerators, dishwashers, closets, or cabinets. Adventurous ferrets have slipped through mail slots. That is why owners learn to ferret-proof their homes. They shut doors, tape openings, and never do the laundry or take out the garbage without checking for a hiding ferret.

Ferrets love to romp, run, and jump. They will run backwards, tumble over, and shake their heads. Hide-and-seek is a favorite ferret game. They will give you a merry game of tag around the house. They like baby toys or kitten toys that move, roll, bounce, or squeak.

Ferrets love attention. Petting and cuddling helps them be good pets. Ferrets need to be held with a firm (not too tight) grip, because they can be slippery. A sleepy ferret can be cranky, so it should be handled only when it is fully awake.

The owner's voice and hands are the best training aids. A quiet approach and soft voice are best. When ferrets get excited or frightened, they show it. They arch their backs and make angry noises. Playful biting and mock combat are normal ferret behavior. If biting or nipping gets too rough, a firm "no" and thump on its nose with a forefinger can train it to stop.

Care and feeding

A ferret needs a special nesting spot. It needs space for playing, exercising, feeding, and sleeping, and it needs a litter pan. A large wire cage can provide these. An aquarium, or a small room in the house that has been ferret-proofed, also works.

Some ferret owners restrict their pets to one room. They provide a litter pan, food, and a bed. A plastic dishpan with blankets or towels makes a good bed. Bedding should be washed regularly. If the ferret is allowed to run freely in the house, more than one litter pan helps avoid messes.

Every ferret has an odor. Many ferret owners pay extra to have the ferret's anal scent glands surgically removed. (This is called *descenting*.) Females should be *spayed* to save their lives, and males should be *neutered* to decrease their aggressiveness and odor. (Females can die if left in *heat* during the entire breeding season. They must be spayed or kept continuously bred.)

A ferret also needs a yearly visit to the veterinarian. Rabies shots, canine distemper shots, and a checkup are part of ferret care.

Ferrets feel secure when they are fed in the same place and at the same time every day. Ferrets have small stomachs. It is best to leave their food and a constant supply of fresh water out at all times. A good diet for ferrets is high in protein. Specially prepared ferret food is available from pet stores. A high-quality dry kitten food is also good.

Like humans, ferrets enjoy variety in their diets. Raisins, carrots, celery, and shrimp are tasty treats. All food should be washed and cut up in small pieces. Ice cream, cheese, and other dairy products can cause problems for ferrets.

A word of caution

Some experts say that sharp-toothed ferrets do not make safe pets. The *Journal of the American Medical Association* has reported a few ferret attacks on young children. One doctor thinks ferrets may attack babies because they are drawn to the smell of milk. In the wild, ferrets are known to prey on young animals still nursing on their mother's milk. Babies or young children should not be left unsupervised with them or any other pet.

Ferret owners claim the animals are gentle. Most states have always grouped ferrets with pets such as cats and dogs. They have no separate rules or laws for ferrets. However, at least three states—California, New Hampshire, and Georgia—have banned the sale of ferrets as pets because of possible safety risks to humans. New York City and Washington, D.C., also have laws against the sale of ferrets as pets.

The survival of the black-footed ferret depends on the round-the-clock care of the Wyoming researchers.

If you think a ferret is the pet for you, talk it over with trusted adults. Ferret clubs and shows help owners learn more about ferret pets. A ferret is fun. It requires care and time from human keepers. If you take good care of it, your ferret will love you in return.

Pet ferrets are a source of personal enjoyment. However, they are *not* and *cannot* become wild black-footed ferrets. It is very important that pet ferrets *never* be released into the wild. They may not survive the wild. If they do, they may breed with our rarest mammal and create hybrids.

Pet ferrets can give their owners a lot of enjoyment, but they cannot replace the world's rarest mammal, the black-footed ferret. Its survival depends on researchers working around the clock to save the black-footed ferret for future generations.

INDEX/GLOSSARY: